BODIES OF WATER
AND
NEW YORK CITY'S
COMMUNITIES

ANDREW MOORE

Rosen
Classroom

New York City has water almost everywhere you look! A lot of water in one place is called a body of water.

New York City has many rivers, **bays**, **creeks**, and **harbors**. New York City has a **coast** along the **Atlantic Ocean**.

New York City's communities often grew because they were near bodies of water. Water is important for health, **trade**, and **communication**. People cannot live without water.

The Lenape Native Americans chose to live in what are now called the five **boroughs** of New York City because there are many islands surrounded by water. These were good places to fish and find **oysters**. These were also good places to hunt because many animals live near water.

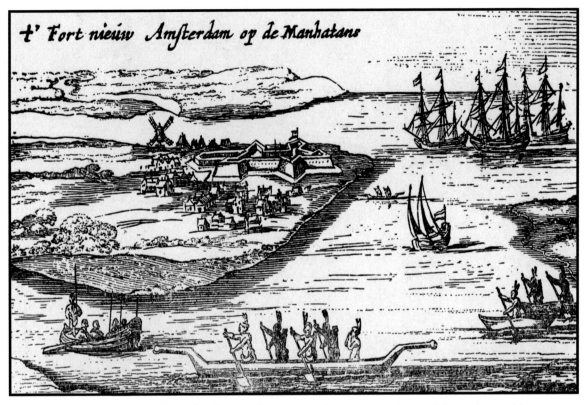

t' Fort nieuw Amsterdam op de Manhatans

In 1625, the Dutch chose to make their city, New Amsterdam, at the tip of Manhattan Island. They chose this place because here the Hudson River runs into New York Bay. The Dutch were able to sail from the bay into the Atlantic Ocean and across to **Europe**.

Today, there are many communities along the shore of the Hudson River. People like to live in apartments on the Upper West Side to look at the beauty of the river. Tourists like to visit New York City on big ships that **dock** at **Piers** 88, 90, and 92. Many people work near the piers.

The East River separates the boroughs of Manhattan and the Bronx from Long Island. When the Dutch settlers bought land from the Lenape, they liked to be near this river. The neighborhood of Long Island City in the borough of Queens grew along this river.

Jamaica Bay is a body of water in the boroughs of Brooklyn and Queens. More than 300 types of fish and birds live there. Many people from the communities nearby go there to be **outdoors**. The planes of John F. Kennedy Airport fly over Jamaica Bay.

In 1849, people dug out the Gowanus Creek to turn it into a **canal**. The trade that grew from the boats that went up the canal helped create the communities of South Brooklyn. Many **factories** and homes were built along the canal.

New Yorkers love to be near the water. Some like to go to the **boardwalk** on Coney Island to be near the Atlantic Ocean. Some like to be on a boat in the harbor of City Island. New York City needs all these bodies of water to be New York City.

Glossary

Atlantic Ocean: a large body of water separating South America and North America from Europe and Africa

bays: bodies of water that are mostly surrounded by land

boardwalk: a walkway made of wood

boroughs: the five main parts of New York City

canal: a man-made waterway

coast: the place where the land and ocean meet

communication: the way we share information

community: a group of people who live and work together

creeks: small streams

dock: to park or stop a boat

Europe: one of the seven major landmasses of Earth

factories: places where things are made

harbors: safe bodies of water deep enough for ships to rest

outdoors: outside

oysters: an animal without a backbone that lives in a shell

piers: places where boats can park

trade: business